THE VERY HUNGRY CATERPILLAR

by Eric Carle

PUFFIN BOOKS

For my sister Christa

In the light of the moon
a little egg lay on a leaf.

One Sunday morning the warm sun came up and—pop!—out of the egg
came a tiny and very hungry caterpillar.

He started to look for some food.

On Thursday
he ate through
four strawberries,
but he was still
hungry.

On Friday
he ate through
five oranges,
but he was still
hungry.

On Saturday
he ate through
one piece of
chocolate cake, one ice-cream cone, one pickle, one slice of Swiss cheese, one slice of salami,

one lollipop, one piece of cherry pie, one sausage, one cupcake, and one slice of watermelon.

That night he had a stomachache!

The next day was Sunday again.
The caterpillar ate through
one nice green leaf,
and after that he felt
much better.

Now he wasn't hungry any more—and he wasn't a little caterpillar any more.
He was a big, fat caterpillar.

He built a small house, called a cocoon, around himself. He stayed inside for
more than two weeks. Then he nibbled a hole in the cocoon, pushed his way out and ...

he was a beautiful butterfly!

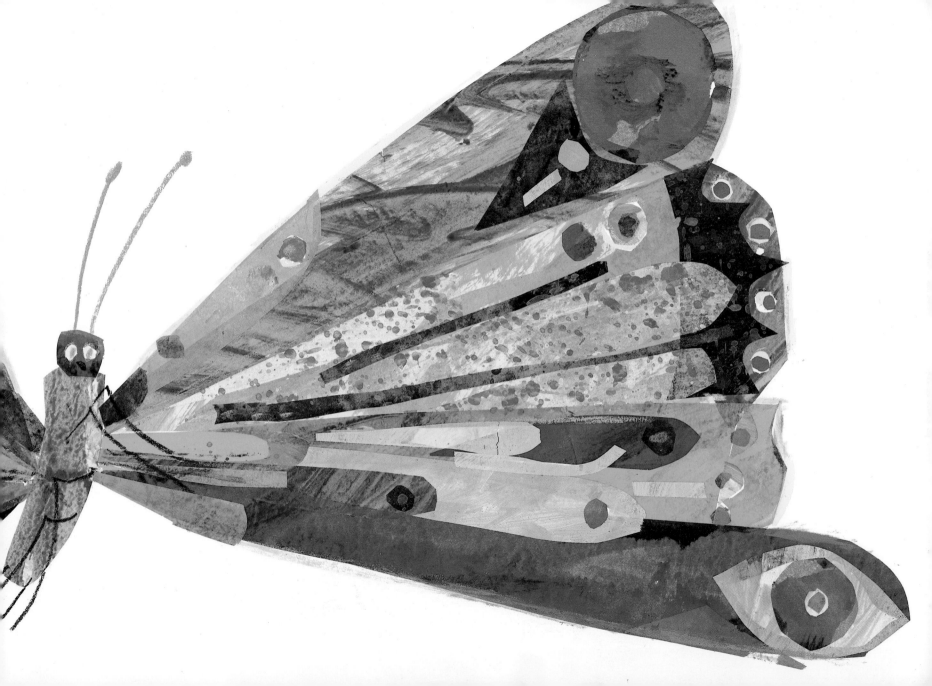